Door to Door

Autumn Leigh

NEIGHBORHOOD READERS

Rosen Classroom Books & Materials™

New York

I am a mail person.

3

I have a letter for Mr. Dog.

I have a letter for Mrs. Bird.

I have a letter for Miss Squirrel.

I have a letter for Mr. Ant.

I have a letter for the Bee family.